CW00394004

FLY

HIGH FOREST FARM

SALLY MARSH

This book is dedicated to my daughter Gemma, who inspires me always. x

The arena was electric, and every step Jenna and Snow Prince took made the hair on the back of her neck stand up just a little higher. Through fumbling fingers Jenna shortened her reins just a little more, her heart was beating so fast she was sure it would soon burst through her chest.

Snow Prince could feel her nerves and began to jog sideways, flicking his head as he went.

"Easy boy." Jenna whispered, the words catching on her dry lips. "We can do this, together."

As the tannoy system crackled into life and announced their names to the growing crowd of on lookers, Jenna urged the gelding into a steady trot and as they broke into a collected canter the sharp trill of a bell signalled that they could start their jumping round. With her eyes firmly fixed on the first fence, Jenna held her breath.

Snow Prince needed no more encouragement as his ears pricked forward and his pace quickened. They were all that stood between their team standing a chance of winning the cup and going home with nothing. The pressure felt immense especially as Snow Prince was so new to jumping. They just had to go for it if they stood any chance of beating the Black Vale team.

Her instructor Maxine's words echoed in her ears as they prepared to jump the first fence.

"You are going to have to fly!"

CHAPTER 1

Throwing her curtains wide to let in the morning's bright but comforting warmth, Jenna lent her hands on the wooden windowsill and peered out through the glass. A full smile stretched across her face, the same as it did every morning no matter what the weather was like.

In the paddock, his silver-grey coat standing out from the bright green of the paddock's grass, stood her beloved pony, Snow Prince.

For Jenna every morning seemed like Christmas morning when she opened her curtains to see her own pony in her own field. Pushing open her window she leant forward and whistled to him. The gelding's ears immediately pricked up and he lifted his head, blades of grass falling from his lips as he listened. Whistling again Jenna laughed as the gelding span round and looked in her direction, neighing in response to her. It was the same every morning and after throwing on some jeans and a vest top Jenna skipped her way downstairs.

Grabbing an apple from the fruit bowl on the kitchen table she ran barefoot down to the paddock gate where the pony stood awaiting her arrival with his breakfast. He really was the most beautiful animal she had ever seen and as he devoured the apple in lip smacking relish, she smoothed the long forelock that reached half way down his silk like face.

They had both built up such a bond in the time since he had first arrived from the auction, half wild and mistreated. He still had his moments and there was still an air of wildness about him, but he trusted Jenna and she trusted him in return. Jenna had spent hours just sat in the field with him when he first arrived and within a week he would follow her around and allow her to stroke his face in return for a carrot or two.

With the help of Victoria and Zoe they had slowly got him leading and tying up to be groomed, and once he learnt that they meant him no harm his progress to a ridden pony had gone pretty quickly and smoothly.

The first time Jenna sat on his back and felt him move beneath her as he moved was one of the most incredible things she had ever experienced. But along with the high moments had come the low ones, Snow Prince could really buck!

He was a quick thinking animal and found the thought of going up a pace very exciting. But with a bit of determination and Jenna being just as stubborn as him, they soon had him hacking out alongside Zoe and her pony Flame.

Six months had soon passed by and with Jenna now feeling that both she and Snow Prince were ready for something more challenging, she had booked a schooling lesson with Fliss Hampton, a local trainer who came highly recommended. Jenna had heard that Fliss was a tough trainer but really had a way with horses; she really hoped that Snow Prince wouldn't play the clown today and embarrass her. Fliss's yard was a 20 minute hack from home and Jenna hoped it would be enough of a work out to take the edge off the spirited gelding.

Arriving ten minutes early for her lesson Jenna surveyed the immaculate yard, with its white washed walls and colourful hanging baskets, it was like one from a film set.

"You must be Jenna?" The voice made Jenna jump slightly and as she pulled Snow Prince to a halt a tall woman, wearing a green polo top, beige jodhpurs and long brown riding boots appeared from one of the stables, broom in hand.

"Hi, yes, that's me" Jenna smiled nervously.

"I'm Fliss, we spoke on the phone. What a beautiful pony you have" The woman replied as she approached Snow Prince and smoothed his neck.

"Thank you" Jenna beamed. "I'm not sure how he will behave today though. He can be a bit naughty!"

Fliss laughed a little and patted the gelding's neck. "Typical pony then!" she laughed. "Why don't you both head up to the sand school and get your bearings while I finish up here? I will meet you there in five minutes, OK?"

The sand school where Jenna was to have her lesson seemed huge. Long mirrors at either end and half way along the sides allowed whoever was riding to see their riding position and how their horse looked while they worked. Snow Prince was unsure of the sand surface at first and half tiptoed and half scuttled his way across as if it would swallow him whole. With nostrils flared wide he observed the mirrors with great curiosity before stopping to admire himself in them.

"Even he knows he's beautiful" Fliss laughed as she joined them in the arena, a mug of steaming tea in her hand.

"He hasn't ever been in a sand school before" Jenna grinned a little nervously. "But he is quite brave usually."

"Native ponies tend to be quite brave I find" Fliss nodded, blowing the steam from her mug before taking a long sip of the sweet tea.

"He had a terrible start to his life, and didn't really like people before I had him" Jenna explained, filling Fliss in with a shortened version of how she had come to buy the gelding.

"Oh blimey sounds like you have worked wonders with him then!" Fliss smiled, impressed by what she was hearing from such a young girl.

"Well let's see how much you and he know then" Fliss winked. "Pop him up into trot please and let's see what he thinks of that."

An hour later a very red faced Jenna and a rather sweaty Snow Prince had finished their lesson.

"Can you still breathe?" laughed Fliss as she offered a mint to the puffing pony.

"Yes thanks" Jenna giggled as she lent down on Snow Prince's neck in mock exhaustion. "I'm so pleased with how he went today, he really surprised me."

"You should be really proud of him and your-self." Fliss nodded. "For a novice pony he really tried his heart out to please you. His walk and trot work is really established and with a few more lessons he will nail the canter transitions. Did you want to book up for next week?"

"Yes please" Jenna beamed before fumbling in her pocket for the money to pay Fliss. "I really enjoyed today and feel it will do us both good to have some more lessons with you."

"Great stuff! Well take him steady home so that you can both cool off and I will see you next week." Fliss smiled and after giving Snow Prince a last pat, she headed back to the stables.

The hack home went quickly as Jenna's head swam with all the tips and words of advice that Fliss had given her. She really had enjoyed the lesson and now felt like she was a proper horse owner having had her first lesson on her very own horse. Feeling super proud of both of them she leaned down and patted Snow Prince's now sticky neck.

"I think you need a wash down boy and some treats" she whispered in his ear. "And actually so do I!"

CHAPTER 2

With Fliss's words echoing in her ear, Jenna had practised Snow Prince's canter work in the paddock after school. Her parents had come and watched her a couple of times and although neither of them knew much about horses or riding they still wanted to show their support for something that was clearly very close to their daughter's heart. They were glad that she had taken up a hobby that involved fresh air and exercise rather than one that involved computer screens, make-up or phone selfies!

Jenna's 14th birthday was approaching, and they wanted to get her something extra special to show her how proud they were of all the work she had put into training Snow Prince. The trouble was they had no idea what to get her. They would have to speak to Victoria when they next visited The Red Fox pub and see if she had any ideas or perhaps ask Zoe when they got the chance. If they asked Jenna what she wanted the only answer they would get would be that them buying Snow Prince was enough to last a hundred birthdays.

That evening, fresh from the shower, Jenna sat propped up on her pillows tapping away on her laptop as she chatted to friends on social media. As she scrolled through the hundreds of daft photos and status updates she spotted something that caught her attention. It was a post from the local riding club inviting people to join up as members and offering up a selection of fun events that it would be holding in the next few months. From quiz nights to Dressage competitions, held just down the road, it was perfect for Jenna and Snow Prince.

Suddenly doubting if she was getting a bit too keen too soon she decided to speak to Fliss her instructor next time they had a lesson. The last thing she wanted to do was turn up at an event on a horse that was far from ready to make public appearances! But she felt this could be a perfect way of making more friends and getting Snow

Prince out to some 'pony parties' as she called them.

Some of the girls at her school had their own horses and although Jenna knew the girls to say 'Hi' to she wasn't sure if she could call them friends. She wondered if they were part of the riding club? Jenna had often overheard them talking about the competitions they had done over the weekends and she longed to join in with their conversations. She just still felt like a complete novice in their eyes and kept herself to herself pretty much when she was at school apart from when Zoe was around.

With her second lesson with Fliss just a couple of days away Jenna had tried to do her best to show an improvement since her last lesson. Fliss had told her to keep her hands soft and allow Snow Prince forward despite him feeling quite speedy already. She had explained that all Jenna was doing by keeping her reins too short, was building his power into a tight ball and that would in turn tempt him to buck. When Jenna had first tried this in the arena she had fully expected to have been cantered off with but instead Snow Prince had relaxed slightly and his strides had become longer and more free flowing.

"You must still keep a good contact," Fliss had

instructed "but you must allow him forward. Otherwise your legs say go and your hands say stop! We don't want a confused pony on our hands, do we?"

Jenna had been so surprised at the difference she felt that she could only nod in agreement but the smile on her face told Fliss everything she wanted to know.

It was amazing how much could be learnt in an hour long lesson and Jenna was soaking up the words of advice and tips Fliss gave like a sponge. She really wanted to improve with the hope of perhaps taking part in the riding club clinics and competitions. Who knew what both she and Snow Prince could achieve together.

Laying back against her pillows she imagined in her head what it would feel like to trot down the centre line of a dressage arena or to fly round a cross country course with the ground flashing by under your feet. It was always good to have dreams to aspire to, but she sometimes wondered if she dreamed too big?

Snow Prince was definitely a special pony and his willingness to learn still amazed her. She thought back to the day at the auction when he had looked every bit a wild pony, all fearful eyed with snorting nostrils. He had amazed her everyday since with how much he had learnt to trust her, they really were a true partnership now. He even seemed to recognise the sound of her footsteps even if he couldn't see her, it was as if he could sense when she was near. Jenna was sure he wasn't a normal horse, he seemed to almost know what she was going to ask him to do next before she had the chance to ask him with her hands or heels.

She was sure they were destined to do great things together but deep down she had a niggling worry that she might not be good enough for him. She couldn't bear the thought of anyone else riding him so the only thing to do was to work hard and become the rider he deserved.

CHAPTER 3

The Waters family always tried to have a meal at least once a week where they all sat down together as a family. For most families sitting down to eat a meal together was something they did every night but for Jenna's family it was a kind of rare occasion. With her dad working away a fair bit and her brother always off socialising with his friends, it was usually just Jenna and her mum sat at the dining room table eating together. Jenna didn't mind, she was used to it by now, but she did look forward to having everyone round the table chatting about their day and arguing over the last roast potato.

This week as a treat they were booked in for a meal at The Red Fox pub, and to Jenna this was the ideal opportunity to chat to Victoria about the prospect of joining the local riding club. Victoria was her go to person about any horse related query and although Jenna had learnt a lot in the time she had owned her own horse, she still liked to talk things over with her.

As they all arrived at the pub, stomachs rumbling at the thought of the delicious food that awaited them, Jenna could only focus on the amount of questions she had for Victoria swirling in her head.

"Evening all" Victoria beamed as the family entered the bar where she stood wiping up drink spillages with a blue cloth.

"Hi Victoria" Jenna beamed, itching to bombard her with questions.

But before she could her parents ushered her to the table that Victoria had reserved for them.

"So how is that lovely pony of yours then?" Victoria asked Jenna as she arrived to hand out menus to the family. Jenna's face lit up, this was the ideal opportunity to ask Victoria about the riding club.

"He's great, thank you" Jenna grinned, "I had a lesson with Fliss last week and he was so so good"

"Yes I had heard on the grape vine that you had

been for your lesson" Victoria winked. "I gather Fliss was rather impressed with your boy?"

"Was she really? Did she say that?" Jenna beamed even harder.

"She sure did" Victoria continued. "She also said you might like to join the local riding club?"

Jenna nodded her head eagerly.

"Do you think we would be good enough to join the riding club?" she asked Victoria tentatively.

Victoria laughed and wrapping a friendly arm around Jenna's shoulders, squeezed her gently. "Of course you are good enough! Why would you not be good enough?"

Jenna shrugged, she felt daft asking and she wasn't fishing for compliments, she genuinely doubted if a riding club would accept someone as novice as her.

"I just don't want to embarrass myself by not being up to everyone else's standard" Jenna replied, feeling suddenly a bit silly.

"Jenna, everybody has to start somewhere and the riding club would be the ideal place for you and Snow Prince to learn together." Victoria replied her brown eyes locked onto Jenna's "It's not all about winning competitions, they hold training sessions for all abilities. You would be welcomed with open arms trust me."

Jenna let out a huge sigh and smiled. "It does sound perfect for us" she nodded.

Playfully patting her on the back Victoria returned to the bar, leaving the family to choose their food from the huge choice on the menu.

The following afternoon when Jenna returned from school, she found a large brown envelope on the kitchen table addressed to her. Unfolding the top, she carefully eased out the paperwork from inside and immediately realised what it was. A yellow post-it note was stuck to the front of it which had written in red inked, capital letters FILL THESE IN!

It was an application form to join the Yaldhurst Riding club. Jenna felt a knot tighten slightly in her stomach but ignored it. If she wanted to get the best out of Snow Prince and continue doing what she loved then it was time to get serious. Forms in hand she jogged upstairs to change out of her uniform, she wanted to study the forms and fill them in from the quiet of her bedroom.

Forms filled out and her stash of pocket money raided for the joining fee, Jenna re-sealed the envelope and placed it on her bedside table. Catching a glimpse of Snow Prince charging round the field full of beans she decided she would ride down to The Red Fox pub and deliver the forms back to Victoria. She knew Victoria was friends with the lady who ran the riding club and was sure she wouldn't mind dropping the forms in for her.

The Red Fox was a twenty minute hack away from the farm through a series of winding bridleways. It was one of Jenna's favourite routes and on a sunny afternoon like today it was like heaven.

Jenna had packed a small ruck sack with the riding club forms, her mobile phone and a light weight jacket in case she got cold. Heading down the short amount of road before the got to the gateway that led to the bridleway Jenna smiled to herself as she listened to Snow Prince's hoof prints as they hit the hard tarmac. Leaning forward to open the metal catch on the gateway Jenna noticed the gelding flicking his ears back and forth nervously.

"What's up boy?" she whispered patting his neck to reassure him before encouraging him forward through the now open gateway.

As she shut the gate and headed down the bramble lined trackway she was aware of Snow Prince looking alert again. Easing him to a halt she stopped and listened carefully, trying to figure out what her horse was uneasy about.

Ahead of them, coming around the slight bend in the track was an older man who appeared to be whistling for a dog. The dog walker was using a high pitched whistle which cut through the still air like a knife, making Jenna wince slightly. Despite seeing Jenna ahead of him the man carried on blowing the whistle and walking towards her and Jenna felt Snow Prince begin to tense beneath her. Before she could ask the man to stop blowing the whistle a large black dog appeared from the hedge behind them and immediately started leaping around and barking at them. As Jenna held on tight as the gelding span round to face the dog she heard the owner running towards them.

With the dog barking and beginning to circle them Jenna began to panic and grab at the reins trying to keep her horse still. She knew that if Snow Prince bolted the dog would be likely to chase them and make matters a whole lot worse, but before she could do anything more, Snow Prince spotted the owner running at them and panicked. Having spent his life being chased and roughly handled by men the gelding span sharply and bolted past the dog's owner. Jenna found herself thrown backwards and as she lost her stirrups she knew she was going to fall off. Desperately trying to hold onto his mane Jenna was jolted once more as the gelding dodged sideways to avoid the dog that was now indeed giving chase.

Landing on her back on the hard, grass covered ground, Jenna could only watch in horror as her Snow Prince disappeared out of sight closely followed by the dog.

"Are you OK? I am so sorry." Gasped the dog owner who was now stood over Jenna as she tried desperately to gain her breath and get to her feet.

"I need to find my horse" she yelled at the dog owner and with shaking hands fumbled with her ruck sack as she quickly tried to find her phone. Madly tapping at its screen she managed to call her home number and thankfully her mum answered within a couple of seconds. Jenna burst into uncontrollable sobs, explaining as best she could what had happened and where she was. Hanging up the call and ignoring the dog walker's continuous apologies and excuses that the dog liked to play with horses, she started to run down the bridleway in fear of what she might find.

The Bridleway with its bramble hedge lined edges, wound its way towards a small group of trees which then led to a wooden gateway. There was no sign of either Snow Prince or the dog. Jenna, her heart pounding and legs trembling stood still and listened. At first she could hear nothing but bird song, and then suddenly she heard it, a dog barking. Gathering her breath Jenna headed for the gateway and as she reached it to open it she could see that the hoof marks in the damp ground stopped just before the gate and then started again shortly after. Snow Prince had jumped the gate.

"Can you see them?" a voice behind her made Jenna jump slightly. It was the dog walker; he had struggled to keep up with Jenna as she had run after Snow Prince.

"He's jumped the gate and I can hear your dog barking in the distance. We need to find them now before they get onto the road." Jenna was trying to fight back the tears, but she was terrified of what might have already happened. She knew that the road was only a short distance from the gateway and she was praying that Snow Prince had headed for the open fields which belonged to a neighbouring farm. If he had gone towards the road the consequences could be devastating.

Hearing the dog bark again, Jenna and the dog owner quickly got through the gateway and both started to run towards the barking. As the bridle way opened up and made its way around the edges of a large field Jenna scanned the distance for her horse. Where was he?

"Please, please be OK" Jenna whispered to herself, large hot tears now escaping down her face.

Scanning the ground for more hoof prints, Jenna made her way along the deep grass track.

As the barking grew louder she knew they were close.

"This way" she called to the dog owner who was now talking loudly to someone on his mobile phone.

Nodding and gesturing to Jenna to go ahead he finished his call and headed after her. As Jenna neared the end of the track she caught sight of Snow Prince cornered against the gateway that led to the road. He and the dog were now facing each other and Jenna could see the wild eyed panic in her horse's eyes.

"There they are" she screamed to the dog owner. "You need to get hold of your dog quickly.

My horse has already jumped one gate and he may jump another onto the road."

"OK, OK." The dog owner nodded breathlessly.

As they got closer to Snow Prince, Jenna tried to calm herself down; she didn't want to frighten him anymore. Suddenly noticing a car pull up on the road outside the gate way, Jenna felt a moment of relief, it was her mum.

The dog, its tongue hanging out of its mouth was now laid down, clearly exhausted. Jenna carefully and quietly walked past it and with hand outstretched reached for the broken reins that now hung from Snow Prince's bridle.

"Steady boy, steady" she hushed him.

Noticing that the dog owner had now attached a lead to the dog's collar, Jenna felt a huge sense of relief. As her mum came through the gateway and helped hold onto Snow Prince, Jenna checked him over for injuries.

Nearing his back legs Jenna noticed a trail of fresh blood dripping down from a puncture wound on his fetlock.

"He's injured" Jenna sobbed, unable to hold her emotions any longer.

"Jenna, calm down, we will get him to the vets

as soon as we can." Jenna's mum replied trying herself to stay calm but anger bubbling up inside her. "Come and hold Snow Prince while I call Victoria, we aren't far from her place and I know she will be straight down to help."

Jenna nodded and taking hold of the rein, smoothed Snow Prince's sweat drenched neck whilst her mum called Victoria.

"She's on her way" Jenna's mum reassured Jenna, placing a comforting arm around her daughters trembling shoulders. "Just stay there a second, there's something I need to do" she continued before heading over to the dog's owner.

"I think you best give me your contact details, don't you?" Jenna's mum demanded, "You are going to have a vet bill to pay and you better hope that your out of control dog hasn't injured our horse too badly!"

Without answering the dog's owner nodded quickly and fumbled in his pocket for his mobile phone.

After what seemed like forever, Jenna heard the rattle of a pony trailer and the sight of Victoria's 4x4 and trailer was a welcome sight. As her mum opened the gate so that Victoria could pull into the field to load up Snow Prince safely, Jenna stood reassuring her horse as he shook and shivered with shock. Jenna felt totally hopeless; If only she hadn't fallen off perhaps then she could have protected her horse more?

As soon as Victoria had parked the car and trailer she jumped out and headed straight for Jenna, wrapping her in a huge hug.

"Don't worry he will be fine" she softly smiled. "Let me just have a quick look at him then we will load him up and get him to the vet clinic a few miles away."

Jenna nodded in agreement as Victoria ran her hands over Snow Prince's trembling frame. As she got to his back legs she too noticed the small pool of blood that had formed around his hoof. Trying not to alarm Jenna, she smiled reassuringly at her.

"He has a couple of puncture wounds on his fetlock but hopefully they aren't too deep. Let's get him loaded up and checked out."

CHAPTER 4

The drive to the vet clinic seemed far longer to Jenna than just a few miles. Twisting in her seat repeatedly she peered out of the back window of Victoria's car, trying to catch a glimpse of Snow Prince in the trailer.

"He will be fine don't worry." Victoria smiled, trying to hide the worry in her face. She had been around horses long enough to know that Snow Prince had sustained quite a nasty wound from the dog bite. The area where the dog had bitten was surrounded by vital ligaments and joints and she was just praying that none had been damaged. There was also a risk of infection and she knew that getting the wounds washed out and treated quickly, was of paramount importance.

As they pulled into the drive way of the Green View veterinary centre, Jenna breathed a short sigh of relief. Despite Victoria's cool attitude, she knew that she was concerned about the injury and was now starting to feel sick with worry.

Jenna's mum had called ahead to warn the clinic that Snow Prince was being brought in and as they pulled to a stop on the gravel car park, a tall man with glasses and a young nurse came out to meet them.

Unloading Snow Prince carefully from the trailer, Jenna smoothed his sleek neck as the gelding snorted at his new surroundings.

"Steady lad" she whispered, her voice shaking a little as she encouraged him to stand still while the vet squatted down and examined the wounds.

As the vet stood back up and removed his now blood smeared gloves, Jenna held her breath.

"It looks like your pony has had a lucky escape" he smiled. "The wounds are nasty but have fortunately missed damaging any tendons and ligaments. He is going to need to be cleaned and stitched up and will need a course of antibiotics to fight off any potential infection, but he should be absolutely fine."

Jenna on hearing what the vet had said, suddenly burst into tears of relief.

"Come on you, he will be fine" Victoria laughed, hugging Jenna tightly.

"I know, I know" Jenna sniffed. "I'm just so relieved he will be ok."

As the vet went off to get everything he needed to stitch up the wounds of Snow Prince's leg, Jenna explained what had happened to Victoria.

"You were so lucky that you weren't injured yourself, or that Snow Prince didn't get out onto the road" Victoria said crossly. "That dog walker needs to keep his dog on a lead.""He had already jumped one gate!" Jenna told Victoria, remembering how terrified she had been when she saw the dog chasing her beloved horse.

It didn't take the vet long to stitch up the small wounds caused by the dogs teeth, but because of their position, Snow Prince had to be sedated so that he stood calmly and still. As Jenna stroked his long forelock, Snow Prince stood dozing, his nose almost touching the ground.

"He will need his stitches taken out in a week to ten days' time." The vet informed Jenna, as he wrote out the prescription for the antibiotics. "He will need one of these twice a day in his feed for five days. That should keep any infection at bay."

Jenna nodded and taking the sachets of medicine from the vet she thanked him for looking after her treasured pony.

As they stood and waited for Snow Prince to come round from the sedation, Jenna called her mum to let her know what was happening and what the vet had said. Victoria meanwhile had taken the details the dog walker had given them and was busy instructing the vet's receptionist to send the cost of the treatment to him.

Finally getting back to the farm, and with the evening light fading away, Jenna settled Snow Prince into his straw filled stable. The gelding looked worn out and Jenna worried if he would be left being fearful of dogs in the future? It was possible, the poor pony must have been terrified and who knows what would have happened if he had managed to jump onto the busy road and in front of a car. Jenna felt a shiver spread through her body and shook the thought from her mind. Snow Prince was ok and so was she and she had to be grateful for that at least.

Making sure that he had everything he needed, Jenna kissed the gelding's velvet nose and switching off the stable lights, she headed back to the farm house.

Opening the kitchen door she was immediately met with the welcoming smell of roast chicken and realising she hadn't eaten since the dog attack, felt her stomach rumble in anticipation.

Victoria had called later that night to make sure that Snow Prince had settled into his stable ok, she also called to say that she had spoken to the vet clinic again and the dog walker had paid the vet's bill as promised.

Climbing into the comfort of her bed, Jenna suddenly felt exhausted herself. With a belly full of food and feeling relaxed after a hot bath, she soon fell into a deep sleep.

CHAPTER 5

Waking up extra early the next morning, Jenna dressed quickly into scruffy clothes and headed down to the stables to tend to Snow Prince. Mixing him up a tasty breakfast of chaff and pony nuts, she carefully mixed in a sachet of the antibiotics and with a little water to make a feed she prayed he would eat. Being a typical greedy pony the gelding hungrily demolished his breakfast and checking that his bandage was safely in place; Jenna walked him out to the paddock for some exercise. The vet had advised that he shouldn't go out in the field as he could get the bandage wet and possibly pull out his stitches.

After quickly mucking out she headed back to her bedroom to change into her school uniform and grabbing a banana for breakfast, ran for the school bus.

News had spread quickly about the dog attacking Snow Prince and Jenna soon found herself the centre of attention on the school bus with the girls from the riding club wanting to know the full story.

As Jenna relayed the story to them, they all gasped and screeched, asking questions about the injuries to Snow Prince's leg and asking how scared she was. Jenna suddenly felt a bit like a celebrity, and told the story as best she could without it sounding too dramatic. By the end of the day Jenna knew all of the girls names as well as those of their horses and ponies, and had chatted to them about joining the riding club. She had totally forgotten about the subscription forms that were still in her rucksack and she hoped they weren't too crumpled up after yesterday's events!

Zoe had got off of the bus with Jenna as she had offered to help change the dressing on Snow Prince's leg. The vets had shown Jenna how to change and re-dress the leg and although Jenna was sure she could do it she was grateful for the support of her friend.

"He was so lucky" Zoe sighed, examining the stitches closely.

"He sure was" Jenna nodded in agreement, as she gently cleaned around the stitches with some damp cotton wool. "I can't ride him until the stitches are out in ten days' time, but I don't care. I'm just so glad he is OK."

After carefully re-dressing the wounds with a clean bandage the girls left the gelding happily munching on his second feed of the day as they headed for the house for supper.

"Ah Jenna there you are." Jenna's mum smiled as the girls came through the kitchen door.

"Sorry mum, are we late for dinner?" Jenna apologised as they pulled off their jackets.

"No not at all, but there has been a delivery for you." her mum replied pointing to a bunch of flowers on the table.

Picking up the bunch of flowers, Jenna picked out the white card that was attached to them and read what was written on it.

So sorry once again, Max is off to training classes!
Hope your pony is recovering.
Mr Tranter.

Jenna didn't know how to feel about the flowers and card, she was still very angry over what had happened. But she was pleased to hear that the dog would be going to training classes which would hopefully stop it chasing horses or other animals again.

Placing the flowers into a tall glass vase, Jenna set them in the middle of the kitchen table. It was a small thing but she was glad the dog owner had reached out to her, as she was sure some people might not have been so quick to do so.

Would Snow Prince now have a fear of dogs? The thought suddenly popped into her head and there was a real chance that her pony would now associate all dogs with the attack, and being chased.

Jenna's family owned a scruffy little terrier called Betsy who would shuffle around Snow Prince's feet as he ate, looking for dropped morsels of food. Snow Prince never seemed to care about the little dog and would completely ignore her as she pottered about the stables. Jenna could only hope that he would still be fine with her.

Eating their dinner in silence, Zoe could tell that Jenna had something on her mind. "Are you feeling ok?" Zoe asked, concerned her friend was not her normal self.

Jenna, who had been deep in thought, jumped slightly at the sound of Zoe's voice, causing her peas to drop from her fork and scatter across the table.

"Whoops sorry, didn't mean to make you jump!" Zoe apologised trying not to giggle at the sight of the peas making their escape off of the table.

"Oh no it's my fault, I was miles away!" Jenna smiled, attempting to re-capture the peas that were still on the table.

"I was just sat thinking about the dog incident again, do you think Snow Prince will be afraid of dogs now?"

Zoe pondered for a second at her friend's question, she had not thought about the aftermath of the attack.

"I guess he will be wary of dogs from now on, and you can't blame him for it after what happened to him. Horses are flight animals, which means that in a scary situation their best defence is their speed, so that's what they do. Fingers crossed he soon forgets what happened but I think it's best that we hack out together once he is better?" Zoe suggested, trying not to worry Jenna too much.

"I agree." Jenna nodded. "Would it be ok for you to come down on Flame and we could start going on short hacks to see how Snow Prince acts when he sees another dog walker?"

"Yes of course we can do that." Zoe nodded eagerly. "Like I said, hopefully he will be fine, but it's better to be safe than sorry."

As the two girls hungrily finished their plates of food, Betsy shuffled about beneath the table hoovering up the escaped peas and Jenna looked down and smiled. There were a lot of dog walkers in the area and although Jenna had never had any problems before, she was worried just how Snow Prince would react should he become spooked at a dog again.

CHAPTER 6

On the following Friday afternoon after school, Jenna sat waiting outside Snow Prince's stable for the vet to arrive. The vet was coming to check the gelding's wounds and if all was well with them, remove the stitches. Jenna had kept her fingers tightly crossed that all would be fine and that she would soon be able to get to ride him round the lanes.

Spotting the vet's dark blue estate car pull into the drive, Jenna put up her hand and waved to show where they were. As Marcus the vet strode down the garden, a box of dressings and other equipment under his arm, Jenna felt her heart start to beat a little faster.

"Good afternoon, how are things looking?" He

asked pushing his brown rimmed glasses back up onto the bridge of his nose

"Hi" Jenna smiled, trying to act calm and grown up. "I've kept the wounds really clean and dry so I'm hoping that they are healing well."

"Great job, well done, let's have a look at them shall we?" Marcus smiled as he started to pull on a pair of latex examination gloves.

Jenna led Snow Prince out of the stable and stood him neatly on the concrete yard so that Marcus would have plenty of light to see the wounds.

"These are looking great Jenna" Marcus announced cheerily. "You certainly have done a great job of keeping them clean and dry, so I think the stitches can come out today."

Jenna beamed a huge smile and felt a wave of relief wash over her. She had been so worried that the wounds would become infected and had done her best to follow every instruction she had been given at the vet clinic.

"I would still give him a couple more days of rest before you start riding again but I think you should have no issues with the wounds now and he can go back out in the field. He was a very lucky horse not to have sustained more serious injuries."

Marcus informed her as he cleared away the old dressing and packed up his box of equipment.

"Thank you so much" Jenna smiled, well aware of how lucky both she and Snow Prince had been.

As Marcus headed back to his car and headed off to his next call, Jenna turned Snow Prince out into his paddock. As the gelding got down and rolled in the dust patch in the middle of the paddock, Jenna lent on the gate and watched him. He really was the most special pony and the relief she felt that he was now ok to ride, was almost overwhelming.

She had promised to call both Zoe and Victoria to let them know what the vet had said, and watching as Snow Prince trotted about the field, flicking his head she decided to head back to the house to call them.

As she got into the kitchen and reached for the portable house phone, something caught her eye. Snow Prince was now charging around the paddock, frantically neighing. As Jenna watched in horror the gelding galloped faster and faster and then with a suddenly flick of his flowing tail approached the wooden railed fence and jumped clean over it.

As the gelding headed towards the house, Jenna

raced out to catch him with a lead rope she had found in the hall way.

"Steady boy, steady" Jenna soothed him as he snorted and pranced to her side. "What on earth has got into you?" She wondered aloud, shocked by what he had done.

Snow Prince stood trembling slightly, so Jenna carefully led him down to the stables again and put him back in his stable. Reaching for her mobile phone, she quickly dialled Victoria's mobile number and was very relieved when she answered.

Victoria was just heading for the suppliers and had assured Jenna that she would call in on the way. Jenna felt a little relieved, but she was worried about Snow Prince's behaviour. He had never acted like this since she had bought him home to High Forest Farm, something was just not right.

As she stroked the gelding's soft muzzle as she waited for Victoria to arrive, Jenna thought back to the first time she had laid eyes on Snow Prince. They had been travelling to their new home at High Forest Farm when Jenna had spotted Snow Prince being lassoed by a man in a field, the pony had panicked and jumped clean over a hedge straight in front of their car, a rope pulled tight around his throat. Jenna had somehow managed to cut him free with a pen knife before his cruel owner had led him away and he had ended up at the auction.

Jenna felt a cold shiver spread through her body as she remembered seeing him laid in the road, helpless. Snow Prince always seemed to get himself out of a scary situation by jumping; he had done the same with the bridleway gate when the dog had chased him.

Jenna wondered if something in the field had spooked him and he had jumped the fence to get away.

"Jenna?" Victoria's voiced broke her thoughts.

"Hi Victoria" Jenna called as Victoria dressed in jeans and a pale blue shirt, joined her at the stables.

"So what's happened?" Victoria asked, noticing Jenna's worried face.

"He just isn't right, he is usually so settled in the field but he was going mad and jumped clean out over the fence. Luckily I saw him do it."

"OK, it sounds like he is a bit unsettled in the field by himself after what happened with the dog attack." Victoria sighed. "Let's pop him back into the paddock and see what he does this time?"

As Jenna led Snow Prince out again, she felt the gelding start to become agitated again. Patting the gelding's neck she spoke softly to him to reassure him.

As Victoria opened the wooden paddock gate wide Jenna led the prancing gelding in, and checking the gate was shut released the lead rope clip. As she went to leave the field Snow Prince tried to push his way out behind her.

"Hey, come on, back off" Jenna told him in a firm voice. "You love being in your paddock."

Managing to quickly squeeze herself out through the gate, Jenna shut it tightly behind her.

Snow Prince immediately started to bang the gate with his hoof in frustration. When this was ignored he then began to pace up and down the fence, tossing his head and neighing loudly.

"Right let's just creep up to the stables and watch what he does." Victoria suggested. "He might settle this time and go off and graze."

Jenna agreed, although she knew that Snow Prince was not acting himself.

As they reached the stable block and turned back to see what the gelding was doing they could see that Snow Prince was now cantering up and down the fence line, threatening to jump out again.

"OK, we are going to have to get him back into

the stable as clearly he is thinking about jumping out again." Victoria sighed.

"What's wrong with him" Jenna asked Victoria tearfully. "Is it because of the dog attack?"

"I think he has something called separation anxiety." Victoria said sadly. "And yes I think it is to do with the dog attack unfortunately. Horses are herd animals and that's how they feel safest, in a herd. The poor boy is suddenly feeling vulnerable after what happened. We best go and catch him again before he injures himself."

Jenna nodded, trying to swallow down the lump of sadness that now rested in her throat.

"Come on, he will be fine." Victoria laughed gently, wrapping a comforting arm around Jenna's shoulders.

With Snow Prince safely back in his stable and eating a hay net, Jenna and Victoria chatted about what they could do to resolve the situation.

"He might just settle back down to his normal self but I would suggest that we try and find a companion for him" Victoria said. "Like I said, horses are herd animals and getting another pony as a companion would probably be the easiest solution to his issues."

Jenna felt a mix of emotions suddenly, she wasn't sure her parents would be that keen on getting another pony, but if it was the only way to keep Snow Prince in his paddock, what else could they do?

CHAPTER 7

Jenna's parents were far from keen on the idea of another pony, when she put the idea to them that evening. But when she explained what had happened with Snow Prince and why it was happening, they did start to see what Victoria meant.

"How do we know he will like sharing with another pony?" Her mum asked, concerned that they might end up with two unhappy ponies!

"Well we don't until we try putting another pony in the field with him" Jenna admitted.

There was a risk that Snow Prince wouldn't bond with another pony, but they had to do something to try and keep him happy and from jumping out of the paddock. Jenna was hopeful that introducing a friend to him would work well. The gelding always seemed happy to hack out alongside Zoe's pony Flame and Jenna knew that Flame had his own field companion called Posy. A little old mare, which had been Zoe's first ever pony.

Perhaps that's exactly what Snow Prince needed? An older pony that would be happy to retire at the farm? But where would they find one?

Jenna's mum had insisted on having a chat with Victoria before they decided anything, so after a phone call that lasted over half an hour, it was decided that another pony would probably be the ideal solution. Victoria had offered to ask around some of her horsey friends to see if anyone knew of anything suitable. Jenna was keen to get something sorted as soon as possible because Snow Prince couldn't stay in the stable forever.

Two days later, while Jenna sat eating breakfast with her parents, there was a knock at the front door. Jenna's father had gone to see who it was and before she could finish the rest of her hot buttered toast, Jenna heard her name being called. Brushing the toast crumbs from her top she made her way to the front door where her father stood talking to a smartly dressed middle aged man.

"Jenna , this is Steve who lives the other side of

the village, he is looking for a home for his daughters two Shetland ponies and he heard we were looking for a companion pony." Her dad informed her; a polite smile pinned on his face.

"Two ponies?" Jenna asked, thinking she had misheard what her dad had said.

"Yes two, my daughter had them as pets but she is off to university this year and I won't have time to look after them as I work away a lot. My wife sadly is frightened of them so we feel the best thing is to find them a new home."

"Frightened of them?" Jenna asked, wondering how anyone could be scared of a couple of Shetland ponies.

"Yes, they seem to like to chase her!" Steve replied, biting his lip as he tried not to laugh. "They are very cheeky but if you stand your ground with them, they are fine. I am a friend of Victoria's and she said you were looking for a companion for your pony?"

Jenna nodded and grinned at the thought of two extra ponies, what would her mum say?

"Could we come and meet them please?" Jenna asked, worried she might be bringing back a couple of tiny terrors to the farm.

"Yes of course you can" Steve replied with a wink. "How about this evening, after school?"

"Perfect , what's your address." Jenna beamed, scrabbling for a pen and paper from the hall table as she tried to contain her excitement.

With Steve's address scribbled down and pinned to the kitchen noticeboard, Jenna hurried to get ready for school and couldn't wait to get on the bus to tell Zoe about the Shetlands

Straight after school, Jenna hurried her less than enthusiastic parents into the car. Her mum had taken some persuading but had agreed to meet the Shetlands. With Steve's address in hand they headed to meet the ponies. All Jenna knew was that they were both geldings and were 8 years old; she didn't even know what colour they were, not that it mattered.

Steve's house was huge! Its winding driveway wove its way through an immaculate lawn and up to a front door that was framed by two huge white pillars and a huge Wisteria tree which hugged the house with its beautiful lilac flowers.

"Wow" Jenna sighed as her dad eased the car to a stop on the deep gravel driveway.

As they stepped from the car the front door was opened by a neatly dressed woman with long blonde hair that flowed over her shoulders.

"Hello, you must be Jenna?" she asked in a soft voice. "I'm Nancy, Steve's wife" she added, holding out her hand for Jenna and her parents to shake.

After Jenna had introduced her parents, Steve appeared at the door clutching a couple of head collars and a bag of carrots. "Are you ready to meet our boys then?" He laughed and as Jenna eagerly nodded, he guided them through a gated arch way by the side of the house.

As they chatted about the Shetlands Jenna noticed Nancy do a little shiver. "I hear you aren't too keen on the ponies?" Jenna smiled.

Nancy did a little laugh and shook her head. "They are pretty naughty, and they know I'm not a horsey person so they seem to think it's fun to chase me!"

"Oh no!" Jenna giggled hoping she didn't come across as rude. "I'm sorry but I've heard Shetland ponies can have big personalities. They probably think it's a great game!"

"I'm sure they do" Nancy laughed. "I feel really silly being scared of them but I'm just not confident around ponies"

The Shetland ponies were shut in a stable on a small yard at the back of the house. Jenna could just about see their noses poking up above the wooden door as they heard people approaching.

As Jenna and her parents peered over the door they were met by the sight of two beautiful black and white Shetlands, with thick manes that almost covered up the whole of their faces.

"Oh my goodness they are adorable!" Jenna gasped trying not to sound too excited, and failing!

As Steve and Jenna entered the stable to put the head collars on the ponies, she asked him what their names were.

"This is Pickles and that cheeky monster is Pepper!" Steve announced as he struggled to put a blue head collar on to a less than co-operative Pickles. "Will you just behave for 2 minutes!?" Steve begged, as the Shetland wedged its muzzle deep into his waistcoat pocket.

Jenna laughed and suddenly realised why the two ponies were so naughty.

"Do you give them a lot of treats?" she asked, knowing full well the answer would be yes!

"I can't get them to do a thing without a handful of treats!" Steve sighed. "They really have got us wrapped around their little hooves."

"I thought that might be the case" Jenna smiled, "Ponies soon get bolshy and nippy when they know there are treats about."

"They can certainly nip!" Steve laughed and he struggled to control Pickles.

Jenna picked the spare head collar up from the stable floor and swiftly put it on Pepper's head in one quick motion.

"Blimey you are well practised at that." Steve chuckled as Jenna took full control of the cheeky pony.

Opening the stable door wide, they led the Shetlands out onto the little concrete yard in front of the stables. Jenna smiled to herself as she heard their tiny hooves tapping away as they led them along.

The ponies although very cheeky were well trained and Jenna could feel herself falling a little bit in love with them.

"What do you think then?" Jenna's dad asked, knowing full well that they were about to become a three pony family!

"I think they need to come home with us" Jenna beamed, hoping Snow Prince would approve of his new field mates.

"I am more than happy to deliver them" Steve said quickly, just to seal the deal.

"OK, I think we would be happy to offer them a home then." Jenna's dad nodded, "As long as you can cope with looking after three ponies, as well as doing your school work, etc?"

"I promise I will" Jenna nodded eagerly; she couldn't wait to get them home!

"Well I could pop them over after school tomorrow if you like?" Steve suggested, keen to get the ponies to their new home as soon as possible.

"What about now?" Jenna suggested, feeling a bit cheeky herself. "I just think if we put them in the stable next door to Snow Prince overnight then they can get to know each other before they go in the field?"

"Absolutely" Steve nodded. "How about in an hour's time?"

"Perfect." Jenna smiled, trying to contain her excitement. That gave her time to get the stable ready before they arrived and meant Snow Prince could go back into the paddock tomorrow morning with his new friends.

CHAPTER 8

In lightning speed Jenna had totally transformed one of the spare stables ready for the Shetland's arrival. Snow Prince was taking great interest in the goings on and Jenna still had a slight concern in her head that he might not get along with Pickles and Pepper. It was too late now though and with Steve due to deliver them any minute there wasn't time to worry.

"OK, we are ready" Jenna whispered to herself, wiping the dust from the straw bed from her face.

She had made a straw bed big enough for an elephant and a bucket of fresh clean water stood in the corner alongside some sections of sweet-smelling hay. Jenna was trembling with a mixture of nerves and excitement, hopefully the ponies would get to know each other overnight and the actual meeting in the paddock tomorrow would go as smoothly as it could.

Heading back up to the house Jenna heard the sound of a vehicle coming down the lane and spotting Steve's black Range rover towing a silver and blue pony trailer, she ran to open the gate.

Jenna could hear the Shetlands neighing as the trailer got closer and as Steve eased the car onto the gravel driveway she could hear the ponies snorting inside.

"They weren't terribly keen to go in the box" Steve laughed. "But with a bucket of pony nuts I managed to persuade them in."

"Have they been in a trailer before?" Jenna asked.

"Only when they arrived!" Steve smirked, "They were really wild when they arrived, but my daughter worked hard with to get them quiet. She wanted to do some local show classes with them, but sadly we never did."

As they walked the Shetlands down towards the stables the little ponies jogged and tossed their heads in excitement. It felt so strange to Jenna to lead something so small and she couldn't help but giggle to herself as their crazy manes bobbed up and down as they moved.

Snow Prince had already spotted the new visitors and was banging his stable door with his hoof.

"Hey boy, what do you think?" Jenna laughed as she and Steve led the Shetlands into the spare stable"

Snow Prince was now stretching his long elegant neck over the stable door, desperately trying to get a look and a sniff of the new residents. He didn't seem to be too scared of them, so Jenna hoped this was a really positive sign that they would become a happy little herd. As they released the Shetlands from their head collars and bolted the stable door tightly behind them they stood and watched as the Shetlands poked their noses over the top of the wooden door. Snow Prince was now at full stretch which allowed him to just about touch noses with his new neighbours and after some initial squealing and foot stamping they all returned to their hay nets and Jenna breathed a sigh of relief.

"I think he is quite smitten!" Jenna giggled, her excitement barely under control. "Hopefully he will like them as much in the paddock tomorrow."

· · ·

The next morning bright and early, Jenna headed out to the stables ready to turn the ponies out in the paddock. She had thought it wise to put Pickles and Pepper out first so they could work out the boundaries of the paddock before Snow Prince joined them. Leading two excitable, cheeky Shetlands was a bit of a challenge at first but Jenna just about managed to hold on to them enough to get them through the paddock gate before she was taken grass skiing!

As soon as they were released the Shetlands cantered off across the paddock looking as if they were tied together. Jenna thought how cute they would look as a driving pair in a trap, and maybe that was something she could look to doing with them in the future.

As she went back towards the stable block she could hear Snow Prince banging his stable door with his hoof in frustration at being left behind.

"OK, OK" Jenna soothed him as she wondered how long to give the Shetlands before she let Snow Prince join them.

She thought about leaving him while she went back to the house for breakfast, but with him looking more and more excitable she thought she best turn him out now before he made his own way over the stable door!

Snow Prince's hooves barely touched the floor as Jenna led the prancing gelding towards the paddocks wooden gate and noticing that the Shetlands were now at the far end of the paddock scoffing grass, she thought it the prefect time to set Snow Prince loose. Quickly shutting the gate behind her Jenna watched as Snow Prince stood staring at his new field companions as if he were glued to the floor. She was praying that he didn't suddenly decide that they were too scary and decide to jump back out of the field again. Snow Prince with his nostrils flared wide and his tail held high started to gently whicker to the Shetlands as he took tentative steps towards them. Pickles and Pepper immediately turned to look at him and in a split second cantered over to him, their tails swishing in excitement.

Jenna could feel her heart beating faster as the three ponies sniffed and snorted, each taking their turn to breathe in the other's scent. In a flash all three leapt in the air and proceeded to gallop around the paddock, leaping and bucking so high that Jenna was sure they would slip and fall. As they flew past the gate as a mini herd Jenna started laughing, the Shetlands legs seemed to be in a blur as they tried to keep up with Snow Prince and his much longer legs!

After five minutes all three stood snorting and puffing in the middle of the field as if unsure of what to do next. Snow Prince, who was eager to have some grass, started to graze hungrily and Jenna breathed another huge sigh of relief.

With her own stomach rumbling with hunger she peeled herself away from the gate and hanging the head collars on the iron hooks outside the stables she headed back to the house for breakfast.

Taking her bowl of cereal upstairs to her room Jenna watched the ponies out of the window as she ate. There was the odd squeal and scamper about but on the whole the ponies seemed incredibly content to be in each other's company and with only twenty minutes before the school bus arrived Jenna hoped that was the way it would stay!

CHAPTER 9

As the summer evenings grew lighter, Jenna started to get Snow Prince back into ridden work. The gelding had been very spooky on their first hack out since the dog attack but he had soon started to relax and Jenna felt herself relax with him. Victoria had kindly taken the riding club forms and dropped them to the lady in charge and with the Shetlands proving to be perfect field companions; Jenna could put the stress of the last few weeks behind her.

With a lesson with her riding instructor Fliss to look forward to the next day, Jenna eagerly cleaned her tack and made sure Snow Prince was thoroughly groomed and looking his smartest.

As they arrived at Fliss's yard she came straight

out to meet them. Fliss had heard about the dog attack and as Jenna filled her in with all the details of what had happened she held her hand over her mouth in horror.

"You were so lucky neither of you were seriously injured or worse." Fliss exclaimed, clearly horrified and shocked at what she was hearing.

Jenna nodded, feeling slightly emotional as she relayed the story.

"We were both so lucky, and I was worried he wouldn't hack out on his own now but he seems to be ok" Jenna agreed, patting the gelding's sleek neck.

"He obviously trusts you a lot" Fliss replied, smiling.

"Do you think so?" Jenna beamed, she loved the thought that Snow Prince trusted her.

"Most definitely." Fliss nodded. "You have a good pony here, that is for sure."

After hearing about Snow Prince jumping out of the field, Fliss suggested that they start to add some pole work and small jumps to the end of the lesson.

"It sounds like he has a bit of a talent for jumping. Your canter work is coming on beautifully and you wouldn't know he had had time off with the injury. If you are happy to try him over some poles then so am I." Fliss grinned.

"I think he is more than ready!" Jenna nodded, feeling more excitement bubble up inside her. She felt slightly worried as she hadn't done any jumping herself for quite a while.

As Fliss laid out some brightly coloured poles onto the sand surface Jenna could feel Snow Prince begin to tense slightly.

"Has he ever seen coloured jump poles before?" Fliss asked, noticing Jenna's face paling a little.

"I've never jumped him before!" Jenna replied, trying to look and sound calm, while inside a knot of fear tightened in her stomach.

"I thought not" Fliss smiled, winking. "Don't worry, we will take it very slowly."

Within a couple of minutes Fliss had laid out a line of trotting poles and as Snow Prince went through them for the first time he picked his legs up high as if he were trotting through flames.

After a few more goes he began to relax and floated through them like a dressage horse, much to Jenna's delight.

"OK I'm going to bring in some jump wings and pop up a small cross pole at the end if that's

OK?" Fliss called out to Jenna who just nodded quickly in agreement.

"He may slam on the breaks as he might not know what to do, so just be prepared for that" Fliss instructed. She had seen many young horses over the years and knew they could be easily spooked by new experiences.

As Jenna turned the gelding down towards the line of poles and cross pole she suddenly felt him take a pull. As she fumbled slightly with her reins, Fliss called to her to let him go forward if he wanted. With his ears pricked forward Snow Prince skipped through the poles and in swift effortless motion cleared the cross pole with ease.

"Wow! Someone likes to jump, don't they?" Fliss laughed, "OK take him through again and just let him find his own way over the fence."

Once again, the gelding cleared the fence with such ease that Jenna was sure he had a secret past as a show jumper. At the end of the lesson Jenna was on such a high that she could barely speak.

"You have both done amazingly today" Fliss grinned, "This pony certainly has a natural talent for jumping and I can't wait to see what we can achieve with him!"

Jenna was so pleased and proud of herself and

her pony that she literally floated back to High Forest Farm. In her head she imagined them flying around a cross country course and winning colourful rosettes, it was all she had ever dreamed of since she was a little girl. Now that dream seemed to be coming real, she couldn't wait for her next lesson with Fliss and to be able to participate in some of the Riding Club clinics. She knew she had to take her time with the jumping as she didn't want to put Snow Prince off by doing too much too soon but she could still allow herself to be just a bit excited at what the future held for them.

Perhaps she could save up and buy her own set of jumps? The farm had a large field at the back which was unused at the moment. It would be perfect to use as a jumping arena, she would ask Victoria where the best place to buy coloured jump poles and even plain ones that she could paint herself. So many ideas flashed through Jenna's mind that she could barely think straight.

As she neared the farm's entrance she peered over the hedge towards the paddock and could see that both Pickles and Pepper were laid flat out asleep, their tails giving an occasional swish as they dozed in the sun. They certainly seemed very content in their new home and with Snow Prince back to his normal laid back self, Jenna finally felt that the incident with the dog was now behind them.

As she untacked and gave Snow Prince a wash down to remove the sweat he had got during the lesson, she heard a familiar voice call out. It was Victoria, who was making her way down towards them across the lawn. In her hand she held large white envelope and Jenna beamed when she saw her, she couldn't wait to tell her about the jumping lesson with Fliss.

"I've got something for you." Victoria smiled as she held up the envelope.

"What is it?" Jenna asked, puzzled as to why Victoria would have a letter for her.

"It's the membership pack for the Riding club, there's allsorts in here, from the newsletter to show schedules. They gave it to me as soon as I dropped the membership forms off, so I thought I would bring them straight down for you" Victoria continued, stroking Snow Prince's neck with her free hand.

"Oh wow that's fantastic, thank you so much" Jenna squealed, she now had even more to be excited about!

"We have just got back from our lesson with

Fliss and Snow Prince was just amazing and we did trotting poles and jumped and…." Jenna blurted out unable to keep it to herself anymore.

"Woooahh, slow down, slow down!" Victoria laughed, trying to calm her excitable friend down just a little.

"Sorry" Jenna grinned, trying to compose herself just a little. "But he was just brilliant, and he loves to jump. He flew the jumps like he had done it all his life."

"That is fantastic news." Victoria replied, a huge smile spreading across her face.

As Jenna, finished tending to her pony she told Victoria more about the lesson and of course the arrival of the Shetlands, who were now waiting at the gate for Snow Prince to return.

"I see they have settled in well!" Victoria laughed, seeing the Shetlands poking their heads through the post and rail fencing.

"Oh yes, they certainly have." Jenna nodded.

As she turned Snow Prince back into the paddock she and Victoria watched as he and his two sidekicks raced a lap around the field before they settled to eat the grass. They really were a happy little herd now!

CHAPTER 10

ONE MONTH LATER

"Don't let her run into the fences. Sit on your bottom!" The instructor's voice rang out as a young girl on a slightly built chestnut mare struggled to keep control of her horse.

Jenna who sat aboard a very relaxed Snow Prince watched as Maria, the rider of the chestnut mare did her best to get a straight line into a row of cross poles set up along one side of the sand school.

The chestnut mare, who had clearly done this jumping lark for many years, had taken the bit between her teeth and was almost bouncing up and down as the jumps grew closer. Jenna could barely watch. She felt herself riding every step along with Maria, whose pale complexion was now going a deep shade of red!

The jumping clinic held by the riding club had seemed a good idea at the time, but Jenna was now thinking that she and Snow Prince were a little out of their depth!

Maxine, the riding clubs jumping instructor was slightly built with short dark hair that always looked perfect, even after she had removed her riding hat. She had one of those voices that made you sit up and listen and Jenna was sure that her voice could be heard echoing in the next village.

As Maria and her mare Gypsy pinged through the grid of cross poles, Jenna began to walk Snow Prince in a large circle. They were next to go.

"OK Jenna, let's get him motivated shall we?" Maxine instructed, noticing that the gelding looked less than enthusiastic. She had heard good things from Fliss Dalton about this pony and wanted to see if they were true. "Let's shorten those reins and get your shoulders back please." She continued, as the gelding cantered a balanced circle before locking onto the row of jumps. "Now he looks interested!" Maxine laughed as Snow Prince pricked his ears forward and swished his tail.

Jenna swallowed hard and wrapped her legs round his sides as he quickened his pace. Trying to remember everything she had been taught by Fliss, they approached the first jump.

"Keep your eyes up" Maxine called as Snow Prince took a stride out clearing the first jump with ease but landing too close to the next making him leap frog over it and the last fence.

"Well done" Maxine smiled as Jenna brought the gelding back to a trot. "I can see he's very much a baby when it comes to jumping, but he is quick thinking and got himself out of that short stride. That makes for a good jumping pony!"

Jenna lent down and patted Snow Prince's neck with a slightly shaky hand. "Good boy" she whispered to him as they re-joined the other riders in the centre of the school.

As the lesson progressed Jenna watched carefully as each rider got their instructions from Maxine. She wanted to learn from watching the other girls and their horses. She knew she had a lot to learn but she was willing to put in the work with Snow Prince and get him jumping the best she could.

As they continued with their grid work jumping Snow Prince got keener and keener.

"Hey, you don't know everything Mr!" Jenna

scolded him as he tried to yank the reins from her hands as he headed once again into the fences.

"Good job Jenna, don't let him take control." Maxine shouted as the pair took on the grid again, this time clearing each one in perfect motion.

"I like this pony a lot" Maxine praised "He is bold but clever, like most native ponies are."

"Thank you." Jenna beamed, her heart pounding in her chest.

After the hour's lesson was up Maxine came round to each rider and gave them feedback on what she had seen during the session. As she reached Jenna and Snow Prince she stopped and placing her hands on her hips, she smiled.

"Well you are a bit of a special lad, aren't you" She grinned, ruffling his forelock with one hand while she gave him a mint with the other.

"Thank you, do you really think so?" Jenna smiled back, feeling herself blush a little.

"I really do" Maxine nodded. "He is a typical pony, quick thinking and clever. He makes some baby mistakes, but he certainly has a natural ability for it."

Jenna was delighted; throwing her arms around his neck, she hugged Snow Prince tightly and kissed his neck.

As they headed back to the trailer Victoria gave them a round of applause, she had kindly bought them over in her trailer as it was too far to hack to the clinic.

"You both did amazingly" She grinned, putting an arm around Jenna's shoulder as they walked. "Didn't I tell you, you would?"

"I can't believe how good he is." Jenna beamed, "he really does try hard for me."

"He trusts you and you trust him." Victoria replied. "That makes for a great partnership."

With Snow Prince cooled off and stood in the trailer munching on a hay net, Jenna started to pack her tack and riding gear into the back of Victoria's 4x4.

Jodie, one of the girls that had been on the lesson appeared brandishing a piece of paper and handed it to Jenna. "If you are interested, we have a jumping competition coming up in two weeks, and we would love to have you on the team." She nodded eagerly, before handing Jenna the piece of paper. "This is the entry form. Just give it back to me at school when you next see me." Jodie continued before heading back to her own trailer.

"Thank you so much." Jenna called after her, feeling a little taken a back.

"I don't think we are quite ready for a competition yet!" Jenna laughed nervously as she handed Victoria the entry form to read.

"Well everybody has to start somewhere" Victoria winked.

CHAPTER 11

With the jumping competition only two weeks away, Jenna still felt that she and Snow Prince were not quite ready for their debut in the jumping ring. What made Jenna most nervous was the fact that all eyes would be on her, seeing as she was the newbie round here. Victoria had been pretty clear in the car on the way back from the jumping clinic that she thought Jenna and Snow Prince were more than ready.

"Like I said before, you have to start somewhere, and by the looks of it Snow Prince is really enjoying his jumping" Victoria had said. "Riding clubs are the perfect way to get started because everyone supports each other. Where do you think all the other girls started?" She smiled, trying to put Jenna's mind at ease.

"I know what you are saying." Jenna said quietly. "But I just really would hate to let anyone down. What if I got in the ring and froze? Or Snow Prince wouldn't jump a single fence?" Jenna sighed.

"But then at least you would have made a start and had a go." Victoria replied quickly. "Jenna sometimes in life you have to be brave and give things a go."

That evening Jenna sat at the kitchen table with the entry form in her hands. She had read it through about twenty times and each time she felt a knot of nerves tighten inside her. Victoria was right of course, everyone had to start somewhere. Grabbing a pen from her school bag she began to fill in the details on the form. The class she was to enter as part of the team was the 2ft jumping stakes, in which each riding club would have four members competing. The riders had to gain a clear round before they could go through into the second round which would be against the clock over a shortened course of fences. The team with the fastest times and least faults would win. For every knock down or refusal time would be added to their scores. It seemed simple enough, but Jenna was still apprehensive. As she finished filling in the form she began to feel a bit better, surely the other girls wouldn't have asked her to be on the team if they didn't think she was good enough?

With the form ready to hand back to Jodie on Monday, Jenna folded it neatly and placed it in her school bag.

Zoe was ecstatic to hear about Jenna entering the jumping competition, her own pony Flame had injured his hock in the field so was unable to be ridden for a few weeks. He had been a great little jumping pony and Zoe had done many of the riding club events with him, so she had promised to help Jenna on the day of the show.

"I'm so nervous." Jenna sighed, "But really excited at the same time."

"You two will be amazing." Zoe laughed, ruffling her friend's hair. "You just have to have a bit more faith in yourself and that gorgeous pony of yours."

"I know, I know." Jenna laughed. "But I'm still allowed to be a bit nervous aren't I?"

With the jumping competition getting closer and closer, Jenna thought it best to have an extra lesson with Fliss, just to make sure they were as ready as they could be.

Fliss had already heard that Jenna and Snow Prince were doing their first competition and when Jenna arrived at Fliss's yard she could see a neat set of jumps set up in the outside sand school.

"I thought we best get you jumping round a course rather quick!" Fliss winked as Jenna rode into the sand school. "I hear you did rather well at Maxine's clinic the other day?"

Jenna blushed a little and a smiled crept onto her face.

"I was really pleased with him. He just seems to love his jumping." Jenna replied.

"Well let's see what he thinks of a whole course shall we?" Fliss grinned.

As Jenna warmed Snow Prince up in the sand school, Fliss adjusted the height of the jumps.

"We will start off nice and low, just to get him going round." Fliss called to Jenna. "Then if that goes ok I will pop them up to the height you will be jumping on the day."

As Jenna trotted round she could hear Snow Prince starting to snort with excitement. He knew he was going to be jumping and was keen to get started. They started the lesson by jumping a couple of simple cross poles and then as the lesson progressed, Fliss had them jumping fence after fence until they had jumped a complete course of eight jumps. Snow Prince was beginning to pull stronger and stronger and Jenna was soon out of breath.

"OK Jenna just pull into the middle and get your breath back." Fliss called, seeing Jenna's face glow red.

"I think he is finding these a bit too easy!" Fliss laughed. You get your breath back and I will put the fences up to height. That should slow him down a little."

As Fliss adjusted the height up Jenna noticed that she was also adding some colourful fillers to the bottom of the fences. The fillers had spots, stripes and even balloons painted on them and Jenna began to worry that now Prince wouldn't go near them.

"OK let's see what he thinks of these." Fliss smiled, she was expecting the gelding to not want to go near the fences now.

As Jenna popped Snow Prince into canter she could feel him starting to spook as he passed some of the new fences.

"He's not so brave now, is he?" Fliss laughed.

"Make sure you are sat right back in case he decides to slam on the brakes at the fillers."

Jenna nodded and tightened her fingers on the reins; she was also fully expecting Snow Prince to refuse the jumps.

As she headed for the first jump, a simple upright, she once again felt the gelding speed up and with an effortless bound he cleared it.

"Look for your next fence." Fliss called. "You need to let him know where he is going."

The next fence was another upright but this one had a spotted filler underneath the top pole. Jenna felt Snow Prince slow slightly but as she wrapped her legs tightly around his sides she saw his ears prick up and taking a sneaky stride out he soared over the fence leaving Jenna slightly left behind.

"Hold on and sit up." Fliss shouted, worried Jenna might become unseated.

Scrabbling to get back the reins, Jenna got herself quickly back into position and straight, ready for the next fence. Snow Prince was flying, he seemed to enjoy the bigger fences and within a minute they had completed the course. Pulling him back to a steady walk Jenna relaxed her rein and let the gelding stretch his head and clear his nostrils.

"This pony is something else." Fliss enthused as

she jogged to their side and patted the gelding's sweaty neck.

"I can hardly breathe." Jenna gasped, leaning onto the gelding's neck. "I think he might be ready for the competition after all!"

CHAPTER 12

A few days before the competition, Zoe had kindly bought round her navy-blue show jacket for Jenna to try on. The girls were roughly the same size so Zoe was confident that it would fit her friend well. As Jenna slipped on the jacket over the top her plain white shirt and buttoned it up she admired herself in her bedroom mirror.

"Wow" she sighed, smiling. "I actually look like a showjumper!"

"You really do" Zoe laughed. "I can't wait to see you in all your show gear next Sunday"

"I've still got to get a few things from the tack store." Jenna announced. "I need a hairnet and some new riding gloves as mine now have holes in two of the fingers."

"Well let's go after school tomorrow. We can get off the bus just up the road from the tack shop and walk down." Zoe explained.

"Perfect." Jenna grinned, smoothing the jacket down with her hands and adjusting its soft velvet collar. She didn't want to take it off!

As the evening before the show approached, Jenna found herself worrying about doing badly once again. She had taken Snow Prince out for a quiet hack and was now washing off the stable and grass stains that he had managed to get just about all over him. His dappled coat really shone through when his coat was wet, and Jenna smiled softly as it reminded her of the rocking horse she had always played on at her grandmother's house.

"Now you listen here." She whispered to the gelding, keeping her voice low in case someone heard her talking to her horse. "I know we are both still learning, but I don't want to look completely useless in front of the others tomorrow. Please just listen to me."

Snow Prince blew his nose slightly and pawed the ground with a front hoof.

"I will take that as a yes then." Jenna laughed,

patting his damp neck. She never thought that the day would come when she would be taking the wild pony they had bought from the auction to a show, let alone a jumping event.

Throwing on his blue, lightweight turnout rug to keep him clean, Jenna led the gelding back out to the paddock. He was usually stabled overnight but Victoria had advised that taking a young horse to an exciting show when he had been cooped up all night probably wasn't the best plan. Snow Prince was already keen to jump the jumps at speed and she was hoping a night on the grass would leave him feeling nice and chilled.

Pickles and Pepper, the Shetlands, took great interest in their freshly washed field companion and began sniffing his legs and tugging at his rug before Snow Prince got down and rolled in the grass.

"Great thanks for that!" Jenna laughed, shaking her head as the gelding did his best to get some new grass stains. At least his body would be clean under the rug, she hoped.

After eating her dinner with her family and chatting nervously with them about the show, she carried Snow Prince's saddle and bridle into the living room to give it a good clean. She wanted everything to be clean, packed and ready for the show. Jenna had written a long check list of things to remember to take, she didn't want to get to the show and discover she had left her riding hat at home.

At 7am the next morning, Jenna's alarm awoke her sharply from her sleep. Fumbling to silence the shrill noise, she sat up in bed and rubbed her face with her hands. This was it, the day of the jumping competition. Her class was scheduled to start at 10am and although the event was only half an hour's drive away, Jenna wanted to make sure that she was up and ready in plenty of time.

As she headed down to the paddock to bring Snow Prince in, her cream jodhpurs and crisp white shirt protected underneath some baggy jogging bottoms and an old hoody, she kept her fingers crossed that Snow Prince hadn't pulled off a shoe overnight. He hadn't, much to her relief, and he looked pretty clean despite his rolling attempts last night.

Victoria had kindly agreed to drive them to their first show and her parents were going to follow over with their car a bit later.

. . .

Pulling into the showground, Jenna watched in awe as perfectly plaited ponies and horses trotted round and popped effortlessly over the practice fence that was situated in the centre of the warm up ring. Jenna suddenly started to worry what Snow Prince would think of the electric show atmosphere.

"Are you feeling ok?" Victoria asked her gently, seeing the colour drain slightly from Jenna's face.

"I'm OK." Jenna nodded "A bit nervous, but OK. I think I will feel better once I'm in the saddle."

As they pulled up neatly alongside some other horse trailers and lorries, Jenna recognised some of the girls from her school. They waved and smiled which made Jenna feel instantly more relaxed.

"Why don't we go and watch a couple of riders do their jumping rounds?" Victoria suggested.

"Have we got time?" Jenna asked nervously, the last thing she wanted to do was miss her class.

"We've got plenty of time, don't worry." Victoria winked and arm in arm they headed for the indoor arena where the jumping classes were taking place.

The jumps in the arena were brightly coloured and there looked to be some tight turns but Jenna felt better now that she had seen them.

As each rider came in and started their rounds at the trill of a bell, Jenna watched on in awe. They all looked so professional as their horses easily cleared the fences,

"Hi Jenna." A voice behind them made Jenna jump slightly, it was Jodie. "Are you all ready for your debut in the arena?" she smiled sweetly.

"Oh hi Jodie, um yes I think so." Jenna nodded. "I'm feeling really nervous but I think I will feel better once I'm on board."

"You will be fine, I promise." Jodie beamed. "See you in a bit; perhaps we could walk the course together?"

"That would be great, thank you" Jenna replied, feeling even more at ease.

With the course walked and with Jodie's tips and tricks ringing in her ears, Jenna, with Victoria's help, unloaded and tacked up Snow Prince. The gelding was quite calm but Jenna could see by his twitching ears that he was beginning to pick up on the show atmosphere.

Once on board, Jenna checked her girth was tight and Victoria helped to attach her competitor number around her waist with some string.

The warm up arena was pretty busy and Jenna could feel that Snow Prince was getting more and more excited, as she trotted and cantered, dodging the other riders as they did the same. Maxine was stood in the centre of the warm up ring, adjusting the practise fence's height as needed.

"OK Jenna let's get him popping this shall we?" She called, knowing that Jenna's team's class was starting soon.

In his usual keen style, Snow Prince cleared the fence in a bounding leap and Jenna felt the reins slip through her fingers.

"Keep a good hold on the reins." Maxine called, as Jenna headed round the ring for another go.

"Steady boy." She whispered to the gelding, her hands trembling slightly. This time Snow Prince relaxed slightly and popped the fence without pulling to hard.

Jenna wished Jodie luck as she headed off on her horse King, to do their round. Jenna and Snow Prince were up next, and as Jenna rode round the warm up arena, she felt the familiar knot of nerves tighten in her stomach.

When Jodie appeared from the indoor arena it was clear her round hadn't quite gone to plan.

"He tripped just before the last fence and we knocked it down." Jodie said glumly. "It wasn't his fault, he really tried hard for me." She continued patting King's sleek neck.

"The Black Vale team have also had one fence down so we are currently neck and neck with them. Their last rider is just going now and then it's you."

"So if their rider goes clear it will down to me to go clear as well?" Jenna asked, her voice tinged with panic.

"That's right" Jodie nodded. "But please don't worry; it's your first event so just enjoy it."

Enjoy it? How was that possible when Jenna now felt totally under pressure?

As Jenna took Snow Prince on one more lap of the warm up arena, a cheer went up from the spectators who were watching the Black Vales riders round. Jenna knew instantly that they had got a clear round. She and Snow Prince would now need to go clear to stand a chance of winning. Maxine, who was stood in the centre of the arena still with her hands on her hips, called Jenna over to the middle of the school.

"Are you ready for this then?" She smiled reassuringly. "The Black Vale team have clearly now all gone clear, so it's down to you and Snow Prince to do the same if we are to stand a chance of winning."

Jenna suddenly felt even more under pressure and she could tell that behind Maxine's smile that there was an edge of competitiveness starting to show. The last thing Jenna wanted to do was let down the team.

"I promise we will try our hardest." Jenna gulped. "Any tips before we go in?" She asked Maxine tentatively, nervous of the answer.

Maxine's answer was short. "You are going to have to fly!"

CHAPTER 13

As the event steward called out her number, Jenna realised it was her time in the arena. Checking her girth once more she headed down the walkway towards the double doors that separated her from the course of jumps beyond. As she entered the arena and heard the doors being closed behind her, she suddenly felt very small and alone. A crowd of spectators talked in low voices as she walked round the edge of the arena and she was relieved to see her parents had made it on time.

"Next to jump we have Jenna Waters riding Snow Prince." The commentator called out over the crackling tannoy system.

Jenna felt her heart pounding in her chest and suddenly felt like she couldn't breathe. She felt totally out of her depth, were they really ready for this? It was too late to back out now as the bell to signal the start of her round rang though the air.

"Come on boy, let's do this." She murmured to Snow Prince and as she encouraged him into a faster pace he leapt straight into canter, pulling the reins from her fingers. As she fumbled to regain them she tried to remember both Fliss's and Maxine's advice, sit up and keep hold of your reins. This was it, and as they approached the first fence Jenna felt the gelding quicken. Clearing the first fence with ease they were soon faced with the second and third fences in quick succession.

Jenna heard a pole clatter but a quick look over her shoulder brought relief when she saw the pole hadn't fallen.

The double was next and the second part had a blue wave like filler and as they cleared the first Jenna felt Snow Prince back off slightly. Encouraging him on with her legs she felt him respond and in a huge leap they cleared it. With the next few fences again coming quickly Jenna had no more time to think and relaxed her reins slightly to allow Snow Prince his head, she needed to trust his judgement a bit now.

As the last fence loomed before them, an up to

height jump of three bright red planks, Jenna held her breath and in a flash, they were over it. Jenna took another quick look over her shoulder and realising they had got a clear round she flung her arms around Snow Prince's neck as he came back to a walk. They had done it! The crowd led by Victoria and her parents broke into a deafening applause and as Jenna rode out through the wooden double doors she saw Zoe, Jodie and her parents running towards them. They had been watching from side lines and could hardly contain their excitement.

"You did it, you got clear!" Zoe squealed patting her friend's leg as if she were a horse.

"I can't believe he jumped clear." Jenna beamed, suddenly feeling a bit emotional.

As they continued back to the trailer her parents and Victoria joined them, they were all laughing and smiling and as Jenna dismounted her parents embraced her in a huge hug.

"You did amazing Jenna, we are so proud." Her Mum told her, her eyes brimming with tears. "We really are."

With Snow Prince untacked and back on the trailer enjoying a well-deserved hay net, Jenna quickly unfastened and removed her riding hat and back protector.

"Yuck!" she laughed as she tried to run her fingers through her now sweaty hair. "I can still feel my legs shaking, I've never been so nervous."

"You should be so proud of yourself and your pony." A voice said behind her, it was Maxine. "For a very novice pony and rider you have done really well. I told you to fly and you literally did, well-done." Maxine smiled, ruffling Snow Prince's fore-lock. "We are neck and neck with the Black Vale team now, so it will all be down to the fastest round."

Jenna hadn't thought about the time, all she was focused on was getting over each fence clear. Never would she have dreamed that she would go clear at her first go at show jumping.

"We couldn't have done it without the support of everyone and of course my amazing instructors." Jenna smiled shyly. "I'm so proud of Snow Prince, he just flew!"

"They are about to announce the results." A steward shouted from the warm up arena.

Jenna felt her stomach flip again; would she

have done enough to allow the Yaldhurst team to win?

She really hoped so. She really couldn't be happier with how Snow Prince took on the course and although she would love for the team to win, she already felt like a winner.

As she and the rest of the team made their way into the cafeteria area of the indoor arena, Jenna could see a smartly dressed lady laying out a row of brightly coloured rosettes onto a wooden table. As the room filled with riders and their supporters the smartly dressed woman turned round to face them, clearing her throat as she prepared to announce the results.

"Good Morning everyone, I hope you have all had a lovely morning here at Green Acres equestrian centre." She smiled. "I have here the results for Class 2 the 80cm open show jumping. Which I will do in reverse order."

Jenna heard the crowd doing a collective mock 'gasp' followed by some giggling. She could hardly stand up her legs were shaking so much. As the woman reeled off the placings for 6th, 5th and 4th place the team's riders walked up to receive there rosettes and pose for photos.

Maxine had told Jenna that first place was

between the Black Vale team and their own team of Yaldhurst and as 3rd place was called out Jenna felt someone link arms with her.

"Keep everything crossed." Jodie whispered to her as they held their breath for the results of 2nd place.

"In 2nd place we have... the Black Vale team."

Jenna couldn't believe her ears, if Black Vale was 2nd then her team, Yaldhurst must have won!

"And in 1st place we have the Yaldhurst team, huge congratulations to all the riders." The woman called cheerily.

Jenna stood rooted to the floor in disbelief, she literally couldn't move.

"Come on Jenna." Squealed Jodie, as she pulled Jenna across the room and back into reality.

As the Event organiser handed out their bright red rosettes and shook their hands to congratulate them, Jenna couldn't stop smiling. As the four team members stood proudly side by side posing for photos, they were handed a large silver trophy with beautiful looped handles.

"Here Jenna, you hold it for the photo, because we wouldn't have won it without you." Jodie grinned, handing Jenna the trophy to hold.

As they stood side by side for their final photo,

Jenna took a second to look around her. She still couldn't believe that she and Snow Prince were the ones responsible for their team winning the class.

Snow Prince certainly was the pony of her dreams and as she stood watching her parent's faces light up with pride, she knew that all the hard work she had put in training Snow Prince had paid off.

She couldn't wait to see what the future held for them.

THE END

Other books in the High Forest Farm series:

1. Snow Prince
2. Mystery

Full details of these and my other books are
available at www.booksbysally.co.uk

Printed in Poland
by Amazon Fulfillment
Poland Sp. z o.o., Wrocław

49709203R00061